Wolfgang Amadeus Mozart and Chris Raschka

The Magic Flute

A RICHARD JACKSON BOOK
Atheneum Books for Young Readers
New York London Toronto Sydney New Delhi

Cast of Main Characters

TAMINO

A PRINCE
He is the son of a foreign ruler.

PAMINA

A PRINCESS
She is the Queen of the Night's innocent daughter.

PAPAGENO

A BIRD CATCHER
He hunts in the forests of the Queen of the Night.

PAPAGENA

PAPAGENO'S GIRLFRIEND
(He just doesn't know it yet.)

THE QUEEN OF THE NIGHT

THE MOTHER OF PAMINA
She is the bitter enemy of Sarastro.

MONOSTATOS

THE KING'S MAJORDOMO
He does jobs for Sarastro (not always honestly).

SARASTRO

A KING
He is devoted to a priestly society, which itself is dedicated to beauty and wisdom.

THREE LADIES

They serve the Queen of the Night.

The Magic Flute is an opera, a play
with music, from 1791. It has music by Wolfgang Amadeus
Mozart, who is famous, and a story by Emanuel Schikaneder,
who is not. The story has two pairs of heroes: Tamino with Pamina,
and Papageno with Papagena. They travel in a strange land, through the
night, and win the day.

We might conclude from this that the day, which is reasonable and clear-
sighted, stands above the night, which is unreasonable and full of passion. But
you will see that the magic flute, and we can say music itself (which we need
to be happy), is a gift from the Queen of the Night, and not from Sarastro, who
rules the day. Without the flute, Tamino could not have triumphed. Looked at in
this way, the night is the winner. What is the answer? Which is more important,
night or day?

Maybe the three Wise Boys have the answer. They are at home in
both realms, sent by the queen but welcome at Sarastro's temple. Listen
to them. To win your own true love and become enlightened, do
this: be steadfast, have patience, and sometimes keep mum.

Turn the page to see the curtain.

strange land facing a terrible snake.

Scene 1 continued

Three ladies come out of a little temple and command the snake to die. They marvel at Tamino's beauty and then all three ladies leave together to tell their queen the news.

Scene 2

Tamino awakes. Papageno, the bird catcher, arrives, singing a happy song about catching girlfriends instead of birds.

Scene 3

The ladies return. Instead of their usual payment of wine, sweet bread, and figs for the birds he catches, the ladies give Papageno a rock and water, and a lock for his mouth to punish him for lying. For Tamino they have brought a picture of the queen's beautiful daughter.

Scene 5

The three ladies tell Tamino that the queen's daughter was torn away from her by the awful scoundrel Sarastro, who lives in a castle the next valley over.

Scene 8

The ladies free Papageno. Also, they give Tamino a magic flute and Papageno enchanted bells.

Scene 8 continued

The ladies tell Papageno that he must serve and trust Tamino now.

Three Wise Boys will lead you to Sarastro. Farewell. Farewell. We'll meet again!

Scene 9

Meanwhile, in a garden in Sarastro's kingdom, Pamina slips away from Monostatos, who is trying to kiss her. Three slaves rejoice at her escape.

Oh no! Not Monostatos!

Boyoboyoboy! Monostatos is toast!

Scene 11

The slaves reluctantly put Pamina in chains, and Monostatos shoos them away. Papageno peeks into the tent where Monostatos has taken her.

Faint

You are mine now, my little dove!

Papageno and Monostatos look each other in the face and scream. Each thinks the other is a devil because he is a different color.

Scene 13

Pamina awakes unhappily.

Scene 13 continued

Papageno checks the portrait to make sure it's really Pamina. Blond hair ✓ Dark eyes ✓ Red lips ✓
But she has hands and feet and there are none in the picture. . . .

Scene 15

The Wise Boys lead Tamino to a glade with three temples. One is dedicated to Reason, one to Wisdom, and one to Nature. Voices from within warn Tamino that he is not yet fit to enter there. The high priest tells Tamino that this is the kingdom of the wise and good ruler Sarastro.

Go back.

Go back.

What do you seek?

I seek love and virtue.

Scene 15 continued

Tamino remembers the magic flute and plays.

toot toot

The priest tells Tamino that Sarastro has only captured Pamina for her own good. This is the kingdom of friendship and truth. Tamino's world has been turned upside down. Whom should he believe? The Queen of the Night or the priest in Sarastro's kingdom?

Be steadfast.

Have patience.

Keep mum.

All the wild animals are charmed.

Scene 16

Pamina and Papageno hear the magic flute and hurry toward the sound. Monostatos has heard it too and brings chains and ropes to capture her.

Scene 17

The magic flute charms even Monostatos. Everyone dances. After a bit, a choir of priests announces the arrival of Sarastro.

Scene 18

Sarastro arrives in a splendid carriage pulled by six lions.

Scene 19

Pamina and Tamino see each other for the first time and immediately run into each other's arms.

Scene 18 continued

Pamina has explained that she only tried to run away because Monostatos was pestering her. Sarastro says he understands and forgives everything.

Long live Sarastro!

Ai! Yai! Ai!

Scene 20

To enter the temple grounds, Tamino and Papageno must wear veils, which priests now bring to them. The travelers are about to begin the tests that will make them enlightened citizens in Sarastro's kingdom.

Oh Gods of the seasons of life, give them wisdom.

End of the First Part.

Sarastro presents the case of Tamino and Papageno to the priests. They are more than prince and servant; they are members of humanity, he says—worthy youths who seek enlightenment.

Scene 1 continued

So begin the tests that Tamino and Papageno must overcome to win Pamina and—the gods have promised—a companion for Papageno, too.

Scene 9

The Queen of the Night feels a hellish vengefulness boiling in her heart. Sarastro has stolen her daughter and now Tamino, and even Papageno, too.

Scene 10

Monostatos threatens to tell Sarastro everything unless Pamina loves him.

Scene 11

Sarastro has seen all.

Scene 12

Sarastro will not punish Monostatos because he knows the queen is to blame. And even she is forgiven, because in these temples there is only friendship.

Scene 13

The two priests send the heroes off on their own and remind them of their vows.

Scene 14

Tamino sits down to await the next test and does his best to make Papageno follow the rules.

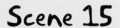

Scene 15

Papagena, a young lady, now enters the kingdom, magically disguised as an old woman. She brings Papageno water to drink. She tells him that she has a boyfriend and his name is . . . Papageno! Papageno asks her how old she is.

I am eighteen years and two minutes old.

What!

Sh.

Thunder.   Boom!

Scene 16

Papagena disappears. The three Wise Boys bring food and drink, the magic flute, and the bells.

Scene 17

Papageno helps himself to the food as Tamino plays the magic flute.

Scene 23

The gods pity Papageno in spite of everything he has done wrong. He will never be enlightened, but he may have wine, which is what Papageno prefers anyway.

Scene 24

Papageno plays his bells and sings, longing for a companion. The bells bring Papagena to him. She warns him that unless he gives her his hand and promises to be true to her, he will be a lonely prisoner in the temple forever.

Scene 25

PRESTO-CHANGO!

Pamina misses Tamino so much that she decides to kill herself with the very dagger her mother gave her. The boys tell her Tamino loves her still and they will take her to him.

Scene 28

Pamina and Tamino are reunited. She tells him, by the way, that the magic flute was made from a one-thousand-year-old oak tree. It will protect them from fire, water, earth, and air.

Scene 29

Now Papageno misses Papagena so much that he decides to kill himself. The Wise Boys remind him of the power of the enchanted bells.

Scene 29 continued

Hearing the bells, Papagena comes just in time to save Papageno.

Scene 30

The Queen of the Night promises Monostatos that if he can lead her and her ladies into the temple to catch Pamina, Pamina will be his bride. Before they do, they are found out and cast once more into the deep.

for Lydie

A
atheneum

ATHENEUM BOOKS FOR YOUNG READERS · An imprint of Simon & Schuster Children's Publishing Division
1230 Avenue of the Americas, New York, New York 10020 · Copyright © 2019 by Chris Raschka · All rights reserved,
including the right of reproduction in whole or in part in any form. · ATHENEUM BOOKS FOR YOUNG READERS
is a registered trademark of Simon & Schuster, Inc. · Atheneum logo is a trademark of Simon & Schuster, Inc. · For
information about special discounts for bulk purchases, please contact Simon & Schuster Special Sales at 1-866-506-1949 or
business@simonandschuster.com. · The Simon & Schuster Speakers Bureau can bring authors to your live event. For more
information or to book an event, contact the Simon & Schuster Speakers Bureau at 1-866-248-3049 or visit our website at
www.simonspeakers.com. · Book design by Ann Bobco · The text for this book was set in Aged Bookworn. · The illustrations
for this book were rendered in watercolor. · Manufactured in China · 0519 SCP · First Edition 10 9 8 7 6 5 4 3 2 1
CIP data for this book is available from the Library of Congress. · ISBN 978-1-4814-4902-1 · ISBN 978-1-4814-4903-8 (eBook)